# Your Favourite
# FIREMAN SAM
# Story Collection

DEAN

# Contents

# Trevor's Trial Run

It was the day of the Fire Station Fun Run and Trevor Evans was on his way to Pontypandy, dressed in his tracksuit and trainers, ready to join in. "I wish I was fitter," he thought, rubbing his stomach. "It's all the lovely lasagne Bella cooks that's done it. Never mind, two miles isn't very far. I should just manage it."

Trevor was so busy thinking about the run that he didn't notice the oil warning light flashing in front of him – something was seriously wrong with his bus.

As Trevor turned the corner into Pandy Lane the bus started hiccupping and making a terrible noise and very soon it stopped altogether.

"Oh bother!" sighed Trevor, suddenly noticing the red light. "It looks as if we're out of oil," and he got out to have a look.

6

"Help!" he cried, grabbing hold of the door to save himself. "The road's all slippery and there's been no rain — it must be oil."

Just as he was wondering what to do next, Trevor heard the sound of an engine. "That's a bit of luck," he thought. "If I can get a lift into Pontypandy I'll still be in time for the run."

Trevor was standing at the side of the road waving his handkerchief when Fireman Sam and Fireman Elvis Cridlington came round the corner in Jupiter, on their way back to the fire station after a call.

"There's someone waving," said Fireman Sam, slowing down. "Looks like Trevor, we'd better stop and help." But as he braked, Jupiter's tyres slid on the oily road and they started to skid.

"Watch out, Trevor," cried Elvis, closing his eyes as they skidded across the road, narrowly missing the bus. There was a thud and Jupiter came to a halt.

"You can open your eyes now, Elvis," said Fireman Sam. "There's no harm done, but I think we're stuck in the ditch. I didn't know the lane was so slippery. Come on, let's get out."

Pale and shaken, Elvis and Fireman Sam climbed out of Jupiter and had a look around.

"Phew, that was a near miss!" said Trevor, mopping his brow with his handkerchief. "For a moment I thought you were going to crash into my bus, and me, for that matter. You wouldn't think oil could cause a skid like that, would you?"

"What's going on here, Trevor?" said Fireman Sam. "Why is there oil all over the road? It's very dangerous you know. Now we'll have to pull Jupiter out of the ditch."

8

Trevor explained what had happened.
"A right pair of engines we've got,"
grumbled Elvis, "one in the ditch and
the other broken down. We need
help, but hardly anyone comes down
this little lane."

"I'm afraid three firemen are
going to miss the Fire Station Fun
Run then," added Fireman Sam,
looking at the ground gloomily. But
then he noticed Trevor's trainers. "Unless," he thought . . .

"Why didn't we think of it before?" said Fireman Sam, looking up.
"Trevor, you're dressed for running. If you run back up the lane to the
call box and ring the fire station we'll be out of here in no time."

"I suppose I could," mumbled Trevor, not looking very happy about
the idea.

"You'll have to," said Elvis, "after all, if it wasn't for you, Jupiter
wouldn't be stuck in the ditch."

"Well, I don't know about that," said Trevor indignantly.

"Off you go, Trevor, at once," repeated
Fireman Sam firmly.

"Maybe I'm fitter than I thought," said Trevor to himself as he jogged slowly up the road to the call box, breathing deeply. "I must have run at least a mile by now and I'm barely out of breath." Feeling more confident he ran on a bit faster, counting to himself, "One-two, one-two, come on now, Trevor, this is easy." A few minutes later he arrived at the 'phone box and went inside.

He lifted the receiver but there was no sound – the line was dead. "Oh no, the 'phone's out of order! Now what am I going to do?" he wailed. "There's no point in going back, I'll have to run on, all the way to Pontypandy. And if I'm not quick the run will start without us."

He set off again, going as fast as he could, but getting slower and slower the further he went. "Can't be much further, surely," he gasped, beginning to get a stitch. "Must be round the next corner," he hoped, but there were quite a few more corners before he finally saw the Pontypandy church spire. When Trevor finally arrived in Pontypandy, Sarah, James, Norman Price and Station Officer Steele were in the park, waiting to start the run. Dilys and Bella were watching proudly.

"Where have you been, Trevor, and what's happened to your bus, and Fireman Sam and Elvis, for that matter?" said Station Officer Steele, looking around. "Trying to get out of the run, are they?"

Breathlessly, Trevor explained what had happened.

"Never mind," said Station Officer Steele "Our route takes us up Pandy Lane anyway. There are enough of us here to pull Jupiter out of the ditch. Grab a rope, Trevor! We're waiting to start."

They all lined up. "Uno, due, tre, away you go!" cried Bella, and the fun run started. Following Station Officer Steele, Sarah, James and Norman raced off towards Pandy Lane, with Trevor puffing along behind, carrying the heavy rope.

"Come on, Trevor," Dilys laughed. "You've been eating too much lasagne!"

"Thanks very much, Trevor," grinned Fireman Sam, when the group reached him. They attached the rope and with everyone pulling together, and Trevor revving the engine, Jupiter came out of the ditch easily. "We'd better get the road cleaned up," said Fireman Sam. "We don't want any more accidents."

"Wait, Trevor," said Station Officer Steele, as Trevor climbed into his bus. "Collect the bus later, you mustn't miss the fun run."

"I think I've done enough running for one day, Sir," sighed Trevor.

"Nonsense, that was just a trial run and, besides, you could do with the practice! Come along now, one-two, one-two . . ."

# Norman's Spooky Night

It was Hallowe'en and Bella had promised Sarah and James that they could have a party in her café. Everyone in Pontypandy was invited and there was a prize for the best fancy dress.

"Hurry up, Sarah," said James after lunch. "We've got a lot to do before the guests arrive: decorate the café, lay out the food and put on our costumes. I hope Norman's thought of some good tricks."

As the twins were chatting to Bella, Fireman Sam arrived. "Would you like some help, you two?" he asked. "It's my day off and I've got lots of good ideas for a Hallowe'en party."

"Thanks, Uncle Sam," said Sarah. "Norman said he'd help, but we can't find him anywhere. Do you know any good games?"

"Right," said Fireman Sam, taking charge. "James, you run and buy a pumpkin from Mrs Price's shop – the biggest you can find – and Sarah, ask Bella if we can borrow her big washing-up bowl for apple bobbing."

"Great," said James. "I'm brilliant at making pumpkin lanterns, and Sarah's an expert at apple bobbing. Do you know any really scary tricks, Uncle Sam?"

"Oh yes, lots!" Fireman Sam replied.

Sarah and James were so busy planning their party, and chatting to Fireman Sam about Hallowe'en tricks that neither of them noticed Norman peeking round the door, listening to their conversation.

"Hum," he thought to himself, "that's given me some good ideas. I know what'll really scare them!" And he crept off before anyone saw him.

"This is going to be the best ever pumpkin lantern," boasted James, scooping out an enormous pumpkin.

"What have you put in that water, Sarah?" asked Fireman Sam, pointing at the apples bobbing around in a sea of red water. "It looks just like blood!"

"Don't worry, Uncle Sam, it's only food colouring!" said Sarah, grinning.

Then suddenly all the lights went out. "Now what's going on?" said Fireman Sam. "Don't move, I'll see what's happened."

"This is creepy," said James.

After a moment the lights came on again.

"The master switch was turned off," said Fireman Sam, looking puzzled. "Very strange." Then the curtains started flapping. "It's a wild night out there, isn't it. Hey, wait a minute! All the windows are open. You shouldn't open the windows like that, you two, it's a waste of heating."

"But we didn't, Uncle Sam," squeaked Sarah. "It must be a ghost! I'm scared."

"Don't be silly, Sarah, there are no such things as ghosts," said James.

"Of course there aren't," agreed Fireman Sam. As he spoke Bella came running in.

"Mamma mia! Save me! There's a ghost upstairs," she cried. "I've seen him with my own eyes and poor Rosa, she's run away."

"This is *really* spooky," shivered James.

"I don't believe in ghosts," said Fireman Sam. "Where's Norman? Did you say you couldn't find him?"

Suddenly Norman came rushing in, white as a sheet. "Hello, Norman. What happened to you?" asked James.

"There's a ghost in the café," he said.

"Yes, Norman, a lot of strange things have been happening around here, haven't they?" agreed Fireman Sam.

"But this one is real," said Norman sheepishly. "The pumpkin is moving, and it has green eyes, honest it has," he gasped.

"That's impossible," said James. "I left the pumpkin propped up on the table." As they were talking, Trevor Evans arrived, wearing a white sheet and a green mask.

"Well, here's your ghost, Norman," said Fireman Sam. "Well done, Trevor, that's a very good fancy dress costume – you should win a prize."

"No, Trevor's not the ghost," insisted Norman. "I promise you, that pumpkin has a life of its own. Go and see for yourselves if you don't believe me."

"Well, we'd better have a look then," said Fireman Sam suspiciously. And sure enough, when they went through into the café, the pumpkin lantern which James had made was moving on its own. In the dim light, they could see two green eyes looking out at them.

"That's a brilliant trick," said James. "Tell me how you do it, please, Norman." But Norman was shaking with fear.

"I promise this is no trick," he groaned. "The lights, the windows, the ghost upstairs – they were all me – but there's a real ghost in that pumpkin, no kidding."

"Rosa, Rosa," called Bella. "My poor Rosa, she's so frightened of ghosts, we must find her."

"Hold on a moment, Bella," said Fireman Sam. "I think I know where we can find Rosa." He lifted off the top of the pumpkin, and out jumped Rosa!

"I think Rosa should win the prize for the most frightening Hallowe'en costume!" said Fireman Sam, and the others agreed. When all the guests had arrived they turned the lights out and lit the pumpkin lantern.

Everyone took a turn at apple bobbing, and James practised his Hallowe'en tricks on everyone except Norman – he'd had enough frights for one day!

# A Bad Day for Dilys

"That's it for today then, Fireman Sam. It's early closing," said Dilys, as she closed her shop.

"Enjoy your half-day, Dilys. Put your feet up for a change!" smiled Fireman Sam, as he left the shop. "I wish I could have the afternoon off but I'm on standby today."

"At last," sighed Dilys. "What a morning! The whole village seems to have been in, not that I'm complaining, of course." Dilys walked slowly upstairs. "I suppose I'd better have a go at that pile of washing or Norman will need some new clothes!"

"How did we manage before there were washing machines?" she murmured, as she gathered up all Norman's sports gear. "I'll just set this lot going and then I'll treat myself to a cup of tea and a biscuit." Dilys poured herself a cup of tea and then sat down and closed her eyes. "I'll fetch that biscuit," she remembered a moment later, and jumped up. "Aagh! My feet are soaking!"

There was a big puddle of soapy water spreading across the kitchen floor. "Oh no, the machine's leaking," said Dilys, as she splashed about. "Never mind. I'll just have to wash the clothes by hand. These clothes will dry in no time," Dilys thought, as she went outside. "Yes, no time at all," she said, hanging onto the clothes as they caught the wind. But the wind was strong and, as she pegged up the last shirt, an enormous gust swept through the garden, taking the washing line with it. All Dilys's clean washing was blowing around the garden. "Help! Help!" she cried as she chased after it.

"These clothes are covered in mud," grumbled Dilys. "I suppose I'll have to wash them all over again now."

"That's funny," Dilys thought. "I'm sure Norman's spare rugby shirt was in this pile somewhere. It's not my day today. Never mind, at least I can put everything in the tumble dryer. Where would I be without it?"

But she spoke too soon. As she sat down the tumble dryer stuttered and spluttered and then stopped altogether. Dilys tried the switch again, but it was no good, the dryer wouldn't work. "This is too much," she wailed, "all this modern equipment and none of it works. Now what am I going to do?"

"I'll just have to hang them up inside. At least I can start on the ironing – Norman needs a rugby shirt for the match tomorrow." With her fingers crossed, Dilys got out the iron. It seemed to be working fine. Carefully, she set to work on the pile of damp clothes.

"I do enjoy ironing," hummed Dilys, as she looked at the neatly-pressed shirts and the shrinking pile of clothes beside her. "So satisfying, it always cheers me up."

The 'phone rang. "I hope that's the electrician calling back," thought Dilys. "Oh, hello, Bella. You've found Norman's spare shirt? Must have been blown out of the garden."

As Dilys chatted away she forgot that she'd left the iron down. Soon there was a suspicious burning smell coming from the ironing board.

"Hello, Mum," said Norman, coming through the door. "Been doing some cooking, have you?" he asked, looking around. Then he saw smoke coming from the ironing board. "Oh no, fire! Fire!" he shouted. "Come on, Mum, get outside. The ironing board's on fire."

Dilys quickly unplugged the iron and they both went outside. They ran across the road to Bella's Café. "Quick Bella, call the Fire Brigade. There's a fire in my house," cried Dilys.

"Dial 999, quick," yelled Norman.

Up at the fire station, Fireman Sam and Fireman Elvis Cridlington were on standby when the message came through on the automatic printer. "Ironing board fire at Dilys Price's," read Elvis Cridlington.

"Quick, ring the alarm. Irons can start serious fires; the whole house could go up in flames," said Fireman Sam.

They jumped into Jupiter and set off through the village with the siren wailing and the lights flashing. Soon Jupiter drew up outside the shop.

"What's on fire, Dilys?" asked Fireman Sam, looking at the smoke.

"The ironing board, in the kitchen," Dilys wailed. "Hurry, please."

"Don't worry, Dilys," said Elvis, "Fireman Sam's the man for the job."

Fireman Sam put on his mask and went inside. Using a fire extinguisher, he quickly put out the flames.

"Panic over, Dilys," he said, when he came out again. "You were very lucky; there's not much damage but I'm afraid you'll have to wash all those clothes again. The smoke has made them very dirty."

Dilys sighed. "I've already washed everything twice. Still, if you hadn't come to the rescue, I wouldn't have any clothes to wash! Thank you, Fireman Sam."

"Not much damage!" cried Norman. "My best rugby shirt is ruined. What am I going to wear for the match tomorrow?"

"Don't worry, my lovely," said Dilys. "Bella found your spare shirt. I'll wash it again. You can wear that for now."

"Thanks, Mum," laughed Norman, "but I think I'll wash it myself. It doesn't seem to be your day today, and I've only got one spare shirt!"

# Bella and the Bird's Nest

Bella had been busy making cakes for the Pontypandy Fire Station fête. "Well, that's the last one iced. There's just time to have a wash and freshen up." And she went upstairs to get ready. "There now," she said, brushing her hair. "I just need my beaded necklace and then I'm ready for anything! Now where did I put it?" The necklace was nowhere to be seen. "I'm sure it was just here, on my dressing table. Mamma mia! So forgetful, I am. I'll just have to go without it."

"Final inspection," said Station Officer Steele, coming out of his office. "Come on, get a move on now! Haven't you finished polishing Jupiter, Fireman Cridlington?"

"Doing my best, Sir. I can't see my face yet. Jupiter's got to be brighter than a new pin today."

"The visitors will be here soon. And don't forget, clean uniforms and boots for everyone, please. We're on display today." And he marched off to get changed. A few minutes later Station Officer Steele came back looking puzzled. "All right, everyone, that's enough cleaning. Now, has anyone seen my medal?"

Fireman Sam and Elvis searched the office, and Trevor Evans turned the locker room upside down, but the medal was nowhere to be found.

"What's going on in here?" asked James, poking his head round the door. "Aren't you ready yet?"

"Oh good," said Fireman Sam. "Give us a hand to look for Station Officer Steele's medal, will you James. He always wears it for the parade."

"It's no good," said Fireman Sam. "People are beginning to arrive. You'll just have to manage without it."

"I shouldn't think anyone will notice anyway," said Elvis quietly.

"And if they do," said Sarah, "we'll organise a treasure hunt and give a prize to the person who finds it."

"This is a serious . . ." began Station Officer Steele, but he was interrupted by Bella and Dilys.

"Hello," said Bella. "Are we early?"

"Ooh, Bella, you look really lovely," exclaimed Trevor. "Red really suits you."

"Thank you, Trevor," said Bella, blushing. "But I've lost my favourite necklace."

"Mrs Price, where's Norman?" asked James.

"Well, I'm not too sure," wondered Dilys. "But I know he'll be along later, he always enjoys the fête."

"Stranger and stranger," thought Fireman Sam. "Bella's necklace, Station Officer Steele's medal, and now Norman Price, all missing. I wonder if there's a link?" Fireman Sam led everyone outside. "Come on now everyone, we'll carry on the search later. Let's enjoy the fête. It's a lovely day for it."

"Come on, Sarah!" shouted James, running down the steps. "What's it to be first? The coconut shy, or maybe one of Bella's homemade cakes? Mmm!"

The twins queued up at the coconut shy. "This looks easy," said Sarah, and she opened her purse to get out her pocket money. "Oh no," she cried. "It's all gone! All those shiny coins I'd saved up specially."

"You counted them only last night," remembered James. "You left your purse on the window sill, didn't you? The money must have fallen out when you picked it up. I'll run back and get it for you."

"Come on, Sarah, I'll buy you an ice-cream to cheer you up," said Fireman Sam. "I fancy a choc ice. Which flavour do you want?"

Just then Norman arrived, out of breath.

"Just in time for an ice-cream, Norman," said Fireman Sam. "Look's like you could do with one!"

"Fireman Sam, Elvis, quick!" gasped Norman. "There's lots of smoke coming from Bella's chimney, and there's a terrible noise."

"Jump to it, men," ordered Station Officer Steele. "Out of the way everyone, this is an emergency!" Fireman Sam, Elvis and Station Officer Steele jumped into Jupiter and they roared off with the siren wailing.

"Mamma mia! Thank goodness Norman saw the smoke," cried Bella.

"He's a good boy really, is my Norman," said Dilys proudly.

"Come on, we'd better go down to the café and see what's going on," said Trevor.

"Looks like the chimney's on fire," said Station Officer Steele, as Jupiter drew up outside the café. "Get the chimney fire equipment, Fireman Sam, we'll need to tackle this one from inside." Fireman Sam put on his mask and went into the café.

"Something's making an awful racket in this chimney," Fireman Sam called to the others, as he pointed the fire extinguisher up the chimney. And as he did so a very wet and sooty black and white bird flew out of the chimney squawking crossly.

"That's a magpie, isn't it?" said Sarah who was watching anxiously outside.

"Poor little thing," said James. "I should think it's nearly burnt to a cinder."

"The fire's out now," said Fireman Sam a few minutes later, when he was sure there was no more smoke. "Hand me a torch please, Trevor. Let's see what caused the fire. There must be something blocking the chimney."

"It's probably only soot," said Station Officer Steele, "I expect the chimney needs sweeping. But we'd better have a look."

"Oooh," gasped Trevor, as he looked up the chimney. "There's something sparkling up there."

"We may have solved the mystery," said Fireman Sam, suddenly remembering the magpie. "Pass me a broom, Trevor." Fireman Sam poked the broom up the

chimney. "Magpies are terrible thieves," he said, picking up a bird's nest as it fell down into the grate. "Look! Here you are, Trevor, you can give Bella her necklace back, and Station Officer Steele his medal."

"What's going on here?" said James as he arrived. "I couldn't find your money, Sarah, but you can borrow some of mine for today. Yours is bound to turn up."

"It just has!" said Fireman Sam, coming out of the café. "Here you are, Sarah," he said, giving her a handful of shiny coins, "go and enjoy yourself."

"Thanks, Uncle Sam," said Sarah. "I can buy you a choc ice now! Come on, James, let's get back to the fête. I'll race you."

# A Surprise for Sarah

Fireman Sam was on his way down to the fire station when he bumped into Sarah, James and Norman. "Mornin', you three," he said, "off somewhere nice?"

"Oh hello, Uncle Sam," replied James. "We're going up to Pandy Farm to play."

"It's a beautiful day, isn't it? Enjoy yourselves." And he went off to work.

Sarah, James and Norman ran off up the lane to Pandy Farm. "I've got an idea," said Norman, when they got there. "Let's play firemen; you're Fireman Sam, James, I'll be Elvis, and we'll rescue Sarah!"

"But I don't want to be rescued," cried Sarah. "Can't I be a fireman too, and we can all pretend we're rescuing someone?"

"But you're a girl and girls aren't firemen," said James. "Come on, Sarah."

Reluctantly Sarah agreed. "Climb up to the top of the haystack and we'll pretend it's on fire," said Norman.

"I'm not sure about this," said Sarah, as she clambered up. "It seems very high. I can touch the roof."

When she reached the top bale she caught hold of a beam and sat down on it, swinging her legs in the air. "Ready," she shouted, looking for the two boys, "you can start rescuing me now."

James and Norman had disappeared.

"J-a-m-e-s! N-o-r-m-a-n!" Sarah shouted, but there was still no sign of them. "Never mind. I'll just sit here and wait. They're bound to come back." Sarah waited and waited but the boys didn't come back. "I'm bored with this," she thought, "I might be missing something. I'll get down and go and find them." But when Sarah looked down, the top bale had slipped down the stack and the next one was too far to jump to. She was stuck. "Now what am I going to do?" she thought, beginning to feel scared. "What if James and Norman don't come back?"

"Help! H-E-L-P!" she shouted at the top of her voice.

"I didn't know Sarah was such a good actress," Norman whispered to James as they put their heads round the barn door. "Anyone would think she was really stuck up there!"

"Don't worry, Sarah, Fireman Sam's here now," said James putting on a deep voice, "and I've got Elvis to help me. We'll get the ladder from outside and have you out of here in a jiffy."

Sarah was delighted. "Thank goodness you're here, Uncle Sam. James and Norman wanted to pretend to be firemen and rescue me so I climbed all the way up here. Now I'm really stuck and they've disappeared!"

James and Norman looked at each other. "Oh dear," said James, "I think we need a proper ladder, not a pretend one. You'd better go and call the fire brigade, Norman, while I stay here with Sarah."

"Hello, Sarah," laughed James, "sorry we were so long. Norman wanted to go and see the new foal. Are you all right?"

Sarah grinned. "Oh yes, I'm all right, now Fireman Sam's here, that is. He and Elvis have just gone to fetch the ladder from Jupiter and then they're going to rescue me properly! Don't look so worried, James. You know we can trust Uncle Sam. Where's Norman, by the way?"

"I . . . I'm not sure," stuttered James, with his fingers crossed behind his back. "He should be here soon."

Norman came racing into the barn. "Don't worry, I've called the fire brigade. Fireman Sam's already out on a call but they're sending over the rescue tender from Newtown. Just hang on a little longer, Sarah."

"What are you talking about, Norman?" asked Sarah, looking puzzled. "Of course Fireman Sam's out on a call – he's here. He's just gone to get his ladder."

"Well actually, Sarah," said James, looking embarrassed, "Fireman Sam isn't here. You must have heard Norman and me pretending."

Sarah burst into tears. "I'm going to be stuck up here all night and it's all your fault. Who says girls can't be firemen? They couldn't be any worse than you two, going off and leaving me like that."

"Who says girls can't be firefighters?" said a voice from outside the barn.

"Firefighter Morris from the Newtown brigade to your rescue." And in walked Penny Morris carrying her ladder.

James and Norman couldn't believe their eyes.

"Stop crying now. I'll soon have you down," said Penny, as she stretched out her ladder and put it up against the haystack until it reached the beam. "Hold on, Sarah, I'll come up and get you." Penny climbed up the ladder.

"What's going on here, James?" said Fireman Sam, coming into the barn. "What's Sarah doing up on that beam?"

"Oh Uncle Sam, we were pretending to rescue Sarah and she got stuck."

"Well don't worry, she's in safe hands," said Fireman Sam. "Firefighter Morris is a credit to the force."

"There you are, Sarah," said Penny, setting Sarah down safely on the barn floor. "I bet that was your first firefighter's lift!"

"Thanks, Penny," grinned Sarah. And then she turned to James and Norman, "You weren't pretending to rescue me at all. Next time we play firefighters, bags I be Penny Morris, and I'll rescue you two single-handed!"

# The Pride of Pontypandy

Sarah and James were in the toy shop, choosing a present for Norman. "The invisible ink or this?" asked Sarah, holding up a black hairy spider.

"Ooh, I don't know," grinned James. "Norman would like both of those. Let's get him the ink *and* the spider!"

"Hurry up now, you two, if we no go, we miss the bus," said Bella, anxiously looking at her watch.

"About time too," grumbled Trevor when they got back to the bus. "Half an hour late. You're lucky we didn't go without you."

"We're sorry, Trevor," said Sarah, "we couldn't decide . . ."

"Come on, jump in quick now. Let's get going before this fog gets any worse."

When everyone was in, Trevor started the bus and set off towards Pontypandy. As they drove along the fog got thicker.

"Real pea soup, this is," muttered Trevor, peering through the windscreen. "Good thing I know the road, it is." He slowed down to take the corner. "Oooh, hold on tight everyone," he gasped, slamming on the brakes. The bus stopped just in time. "Seems to be something across the road," said Trevor, jumping out to have a look. "Bloomin' 'eck!" he shouted, "there's been a landslide. The road's completely blocked – we'll have to go round the other way."

But as he climbed back into the bus there was a big rumble and earth started rolling down the bank until the road behind the bus was covered. "Oh my goodness," Trevor cried. "Now we can't go backwards or forwards. We're trapped! I wish Fireman Sam was here. He'd know what to do."

"Shouldn't we call the fire brigade?" shouted James from the back of the bus.

"I'll nip back down the road to the call box," said Trevor. "But first, everyone must get out of the bus. You'll be much safer further up the road, and you can stop any more cars from coming down here."

At Pontypandy Fire Station Firefighter Penny Morris was putting Fireman Sam, Fireman Elvis Cridlington and even Station Officer Steele through their paces. "Two and two, three and two, four and two; that's it Fireman Sam," she chanted. "You need to be strong to be a firefighter." Penny turned to Station Officer Steele. "Come on, Sir, stretch those legs!"

"Oh look," said Station Officer Steele, jumping up. "There's a message coming through on the printer. I'm sorry, everyone, but it looks as if we'll have to finish our exercises for today."

"Pontypandy to Newtown road blocked by landslide," read Fireman Sam, "bus and passengers trapped."

"Sounds like a job for the rescue tender," said Elvis, beaming at Penny.

"Yes, but landslides can be very dangerous. We'll need all the strength we've got – you'd better bring Jupiter, too."

"You go with Penny, Fireman Sam," ordered Station Officer Steele. "Elvis and I will follow you in Jupiter." With the sirens blaring, the convoy set off.

A few minutes later, they arrived at the scene. Sarah, James, Bella and Dilys were shivering by the side of the road. ''You did very well to get all your passengers out, Auxiliary Fireman Evans. Good show,'' said Station Officer Steele.

''What about my bus?'' wailed Trevor.

''Right,'' said Station Officer Steele, ''standard landslide procedure.''

''Yes, but what's that, Sir?'' asked Elvis.

''Well then, um, let's see now . . .'' stuttered Station Officer Steele.

''Dig,'' said Fireman Sam. ''Let's get out the spades and dig tracks in the earth so we can tow the bus out.''

''Here you are, Elvis, borrow one of mine,'' said Penny, handing him a spade from the back of the rescue tender.

''Ooo, thanks, Penny,'' said Elvis trying not to blush.

"Come on now, one two, one two, put your backs into it," said Penny, as she shovelled the soil out of the way. "This is hard work. Didn't I say you need to be strong to be a firefighter?"

"I thought we'd finished our exercises for today," muttered Station Officer Steele, wiping his brow.

"Hurry up," shouted Fireman Sam. "There's more earth coming down. We haven't got much time." They all put their heads down and dug as fast as they could. Before long, they had made tracks through the earth. "Right then," said Fireman Sam. "Now all we need to do is attach a towrope and pull the bus out. Trevor, you get in so you can steer. And don't look so worried, a good wash and your bus will be good as new again."

"We'll clean it for you," called James and Sarah together.

Trevor climbed into the bus but jumped out again immediately. "Now what's wrong, Trevor?" said Station Officer Steele impatiently.

"There's a t.t.t.tarantula in my seat, Sir," stuttered Trevor.

"Impossible, Evans," bellowed Station Officer Steele. "You must be seeing things. Fireman Sam, you have a look."

"Oh no!" James whispered to Sarah, "we're really in trouble now. You must have dropped Norman's present when you got out of the bus."

"Looks like Norman's been here!" said Fireman Sam, winking at Sarah and James as he held up the toy spider. "You'd better keep this behind bars, Sarah, or you won't be travelling by bus again!"

"Come on now," said Penny, "my tender's not strong enough for towing. We'd better use Jupiter. Please will you take the wheel, Fireman Sam?"

Fireman Sam climbed into the cab and started the engine.

Towed by Jupiter, the bus slid out of the mud easily and was soon back on firm ground again. "There you are, Trevor," said Station Officer Steele.

"Thank you very much for your help, Firefighter Morris," said Fireman Sam.

"It was nothing," said Penny, looking at the group of beaming firemen. "Without Jupiter and you four firemen no one would even be able to see Trevor's bus by now. They don't call you The Pride of Pontypandy for nothing!"

# Elvis's Experiment

Fireman Elvis Cridlington and Fireman Sam were on their way back to Pontypandy after a fire. "Let's hope that's it for today, Fireman Sam," said Elvis, as they drove into Pontypandy. "Penny Morris is coming over from Newtown for supper and I'm going to cook something extra special."

"Your cooking is always extra special, or extra-ordinary!" said Fireman Sam laughing. "What's it tonight, Elvis?"

"Just you wait. When they hear about tonight, the Newtown brigade will wish I was their cook," said Elvis.

"And so will the Pontypandy brigade!" laughed Fireman Sam, as Jupiter drew up outside his house. "Could you drop me here please? I'd better change if we've got company tonight. I'll see you later."

"Humph," thought Elvis as he drove on towards the fire station. "I'll make Fireman Sam eat his words, if he's got room that is. I'm going to cook something that's really delicious, and very healthy. But what?" Then suddenly he had a brainwave. "Got it!" he shouted out loud.

"The perfect food. I'll show Fireman Sam just how good a cook I really am." Elvis parked Jupiter in the station and ran inside. "There will be plenty of time to tidy up later," he said to himself. But Elvis was so pleased with his idea he completely forgot to refill Jupiter's water tank.

First Elvis made a big salad and then he started on his experiment. Nut cutlets, but with a difference! "I bet Penny's never had deep fried nut cutlets before," he said, smiling as he poured the oil into the pan. "She's going to be so impressed."

"Gosh, Elvis, these cutlets are really something," she'd say. "You're the best cook in the valley!" And Elvis blushed at the thought.

In a daydream, Elvis chopped up the nuts and made twelve perfect cutlets. It took him ages. "There now, there's just time to change before Penny arrives," he said, as he put them carefully into the fryer.

Then suddenly he remembered that he had to clean Jupiter for Station Officer Steele's inspection. "Oh my!" he flapped, grabbing a bucket and cloth and dashing out of the kitchen. "Who says you can't be a fireman and a cook," Elvis said to himself as he set to work. But he was so busy polishing Jupiter that he completely forgot about his experiment. "Penny's going to be able to see her face in Jupiter," he said, humming gleefully to himself.

Elvis was woken from his daydream by the sound of a siren. "That's funny," said Elvis, looking up.

"I wonder what's going on." The sound came closer and closer until it stopped right outside the fire station! Elvis looked out of the window and saw Firefighter Penny Morris's rescue tender parked outside. Elvis scrambled out of Jupiter.

"Evenin', Penny," he said. "You must be hungry. You arrived in such a hurry anyone would think you've come to put out a fire!"

Fireman Sam came running up.

"Gracious," gasped Elvis. "Everyone's early tonight. Well I'm afraid you'll have to wait a while for your supper – but it'll be worth it, believe me!"

Fireman Sam and Penny looked at each other, then back at Elvis. "But we *have* come to put out a fire, Elvis," cried Penny.

"Really Elvis, you're meant to be a fireman and you don't even notice a fire when it's right here, under your nose!" said Fireman Sam. And then he added, "Surely even you must have noticed the smell of burning nuts!"

"Burning nuts," murmured Elvis, going pale, "I'd better man the hose."

Quickly Elvis pulled out the hose. Nothing happened.

"It must be blocked," shouted Fireman Sam. "You did refill the tank, didn't you, Elvis?"

"Oh no, now I'm in trouble," groaned Elvis, going even paler.

"We don't want the hose, anyway," said Penny. "We need a fire extinguisher for this." And she took one out of the rescue tender. "I always carry this in case of emergencies," she explained.

"Thank you, Firefighter Morris," said Fireman Sam, taking the extinguisher. He pulled on his mask and went into the kitchen.

"I wonder what caused the fire, don't you, Elvis?" asked Penny.

"Um," stuttered Elvis, trembling.

"What's going on here?" said Station Officer Steele, arriving at the fire station. "This is only an experimental exercise, I presume?"

"Sort of, you could say," replied Elvis, going bright red.

"Fire's out. Not much damage done," said Fireman Sam, coming outside again. "But I'm afraid whatever you were frying is ruined, Elvis."

"Frying!" bellowed Station Officer Steele. "But I thought I'd banned fried food, on Firefighter Morris's advice. Too much fat isn't good for you, is it?"

"But . . ." stammered Elvis.

"That's right, Sir, it's better not to eat too much fried food," agreed Penny.

"But I was cooking nut cutlets, deep fried, as an experiment. I thought they'd be tastier that way," explained Elvis, looking sorry for himself. "However hard I try, something always goes wrong."

"Or someone always goes wrong," laughed Fireman Sam. "Cheer up, Elvis, let's go to Bella's café and have pasta instead!"

"Yummy," said Elvis smiling again. "That sound's delicious, and even better, I don't have to do the cooking. Making all those cutlets was driving me nuts!"

# Christmas in Pontypandy

When the people of Pontypandy woke on Christmas Eve there was a surprise for them. It had snowed heavily during the night and now the village was glistening in the sun. "Magic," shouted Norman, as he ran out of the shop. "See you later, Mum. I'm off sledging."

"Norman!" shouted Dilys, looking round. "Come back here and help me clear the path." But Norman had run off down the street with his sledge.

James and Sarah were making a snowman. "The finishing touch!" grinned James, placing an old cap on the snowman's head.

"He looks just like Trevor," Sarah giggled. "Oh, hello, Trevor, didn't see you there. What do you think of our snowman?"

Trevor laughed. "Very handsome!"

Norman came tearing up the road. "Come on, you two, bring your sledge. I'll race you down the mountain!"

"A hundred miles an hour!" cried James, and the three children set off with their sledges towards the hillside overlooking Pontypandy.

Up at Pontypandy Fire Station, the firemen had cleared all the snow from the drive so Jupiter, the fire engine, could get away quickly if there was an emergency call.

"Mustn't let snow disrupt us, eh, Fireman Sam?" said Station Officer Steele.

"No, Sir," agreed Fireman Sam, "but let's hope we're in for a quiet day. We've got to go and fetch the Christmas tree for the village square."

"Quite right, Fireman Sam," said Station Officer Steele. "Can't have Christmas without a tree."

Outside the village, Sarah, James and Norman were having fun sledging.

"Weeeee!" squealed Sarah, as she and James shot down the hill.

"Let's try over there," suggested Norman, pointing at a much steeper slope. "We could beat the world snow speed record!"

"I don't think . . ." said James, as they trudged up to the top of the steepest hill. "It's very steep."

"Come on, scaredy cat," jeered Sarah. "Bags I go in front."

"One, two, three, GO!" shouted Norman, and off they went, faster and faster, gathering speed over the smooth snow. Norman was in the lead. "First one through the gate is the winner," he yelled, as he shot between the gateposts. "Yes! It's the gold for Norman Price! Magic!"

"Look out!" cried Sarah, as the sledges sped on. "We're heading straight for the pond." Norman rolled off his sledge into a snowdrift. "Brake, James, brake!" screamed Sarah, but their sledge was going too fast.

It reached the bottom of the hill and shot across the ice to the centre of the pond. There was a loud CRACK! "The ice is breaking," gasped Sarah in horror.

"We'll drown!" screamed James.

"Don't move," yelled Norman. "I'll go and 'phone for help," and he ran off towards Pandy Lane, leaving Sarah and James clinging to their sledge in the centre of the pond.

At Pontypandy Fire Station, the alarm rang out and a message came through on the printer. "Children trapped on ice in middle of Pandy Pond," read Station Officer Steele. A few seconds later, the firemen were on their way in Jupiter.

"Great fires of London! It's Sarah and James," cried Fireman Sam, when they reached the pond.

"Don't panic, you two."

"Save us, Uncle Sam!" shouted James. The firemen placed a ladder on the ground and carefully extended it over the ice towards the children.

"Now then, Sarah," called Fireman Sam. "Come towards me slowly, on all fours. Wait a minute, James."

"O.K., Uncle Sam," said James, bravely.

Sarah crawled along the ladder to the edge of the ice, and a few moments later she was standing safely on the bank. "Your turn now, James," said Fireman Sam. Soon James too was safe on the ground again. "Right then," said Fireman Sam. "Let's get you three warm and dry. Come on." Sarah, James and Norman climbed into Jupiter with the firemen and they set off back to Pontypandy.

Bella soon had the children warming themselves in front of the fire. "These sausage rolls are great for warming you up when you come back from an arctic expedition," said James.

"If it hadn't been for Norman, you wouldn't be back at all," said Fireman Sam. "Snow is great fun to play in, but ice can be very dangerous. You should only sledge where you know it's safe," he warned.

"Thanks, Norman," said Sarah.

"O.K.," mumbled Norman, bashfully.

As darkness fell on the village the snow made everything look magical. "This is a great Christmas tree, Uncle Sam," said James, as everyone gathered round to sing carols.

Fireman Sam produced a large sack and spoke to the twins. "I'm working on Christmas Day, so you'd better have these now." He reached into the sack. "There's one for you too, Norman."

"Thanks a million," they cried excitedly.

"Just one more thing to do," said Fireman Sam, as he finished his cocoa later that night. "Might as well, just in case." And he hung his Christmas stocking on the mantlepiece. He looked out of the window at the snow-covered village, sparkling in the moonlight.

"Merry Christmas, Pontypandy!"

Stories first published in Great Britain 1990
by Buzz Books, an imprint of Reed Children's Books
Michelin House, 81 Fulham Road, London SW3 6RB
and Auckland, Melbourne, Singapore and Toronto

This edition published 1992 by Dean,
in association with Heinemann Young Books
Reprinted 1992, 1993 and 1994

Fireman Sam © copyright 1985 Prism Art & Design Limited
Text © copyright 1990 William Heinemann Limited
Illustrations © copyright 1990 William Heinemann Limited
Stories by Caroline Hill-Trevor
Illustrations by CLIC!
Based on the animation series produced by Bumper Films for
S4C/Channel 4 Wales and Prism Art & Design Limited
Original idea by Dave Gingell and Dave Jones, assisted by Mike Young.
Characters created by Rob Lee.

Produced by Mandarin Offset
Printed and bound in China

ISBN 0 603 55051 7

A CIP catalogue record for this book is available in the British Library.